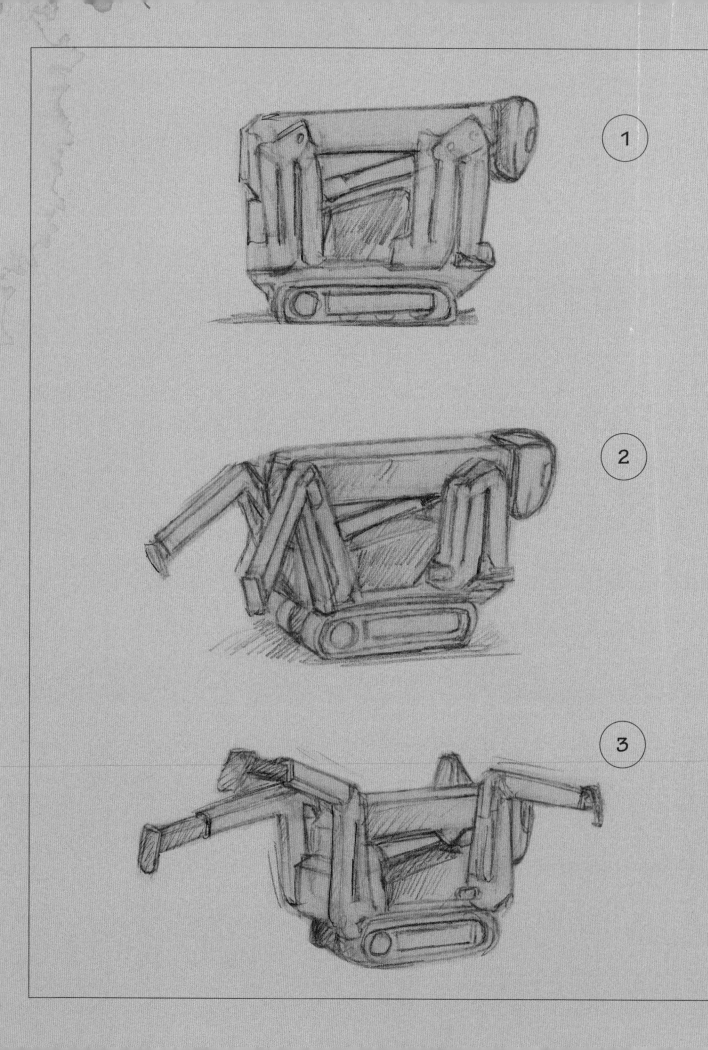

1

2

3

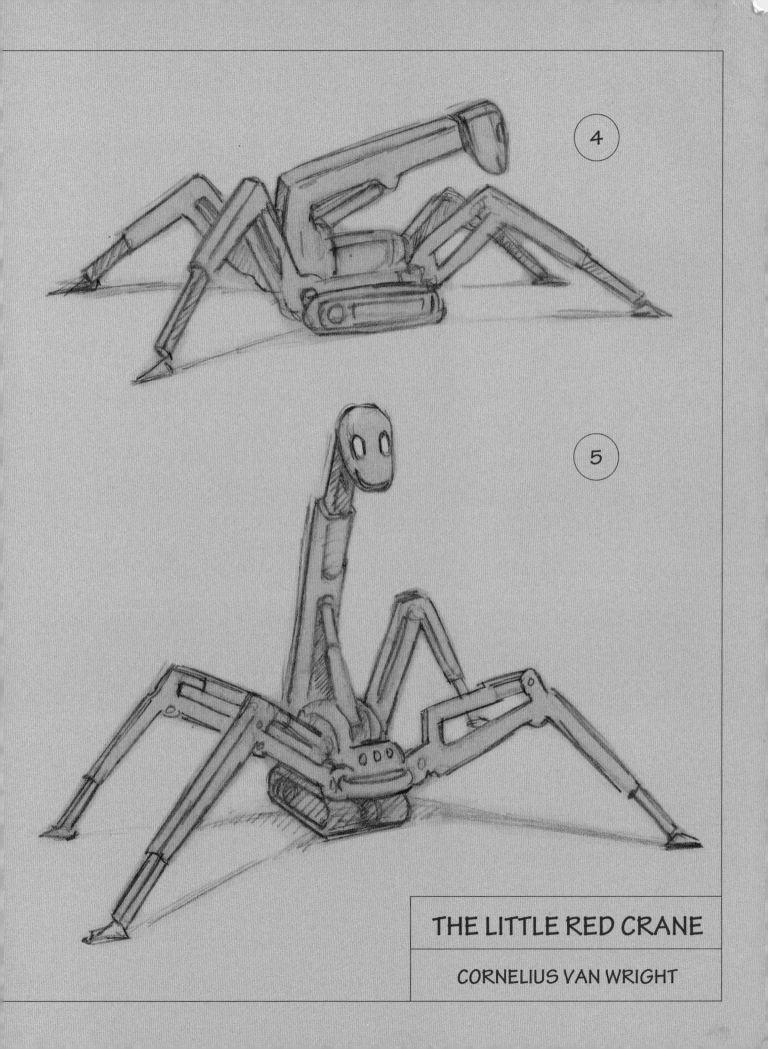

4

5

THE LITTLE RED CRANE

CORNELIUS VAN WRIGHT

THE
Little Red Crane

THE
Little Red Crane

By
CORNELIUS VAN WRIGHT

STAR BRIGHT BOOKS
CAMBRIDGE MASSACHUSETTS

The name Star Bright Books and the Star Bright Books logo are registered trademarks
of Star Bright Books, Inc. Please visit www.starbrightbooks.com. For orders, please
email: orders@starbrightbooks.com or call: (617) 354-1300.

Hardback ISBN: 978-1-59572-843-2
Paperback ISBN: 978-1-59572-844-9
Star Bright Books / MA / 00105200
Printed in China / TOPPAN / 9 8 7 6 5 4 3 2 1

Printed on paper from sustainable forests.

Library of Congress Cataloging-in-Publication Data

Names: Van Wright, Cornelius, author, illustrator.
Title: The little red crane / by Cornelius Van Wright.
Description: [Cambridge], MA : Star Bright Books, [2020] | Summary: As Dex,
  the Mini Red Crane, and his very tall Operator, Pete, make their way to a
  very big job, they meet many other types of cranes.
Identifiers: LCCN 2018055069| ISBN 9781595728432 (hardback) | ISBN
  9781595728449 (pbk.)
Subjects: | CYAC: Cranes, derricks, etc.--Fiction.
Classification: LCC PZ7.V394 Lit 2019 | DDC [E]--dc23
LC record available at https://lccn.loc.gov/2018055069

To Kenneth —C.V.W.

A special thank you to the generous staff of Smiley Lifting Solutions for all their help in learning all about the Spyder Crane.

One day Dex the Little Red Crane and his very tall operator, Pete, received a letter.
"Will you help us with an incredibly **BIG** project?" the letter asked.

The letter came from far away. Pete packed his toothbrush and a fresh can of oil for Dex, and they headed out the next morning.

They didn't go far before they had to yield to a **STOP** sign.

It was because their friend **LARRY** the **LOADER CRANE** was backing into a construction site.

Larry had to deliver a load of steel beams for a new building. He used his outriggers to keep from tipping over while unloading the beams.

Working next to Larry was **TERRY** the **TELESCOPIC CRANE**. Terry took the steel beams Larry unloaded and lifted them high to the workers above.

"Hey Dex, would you like to help?" Terry asked. "I'm sure there must be something you can lift here."

"No thanks," replied Dex. "I'm on my way to an incredibly important **BIG** JOB."

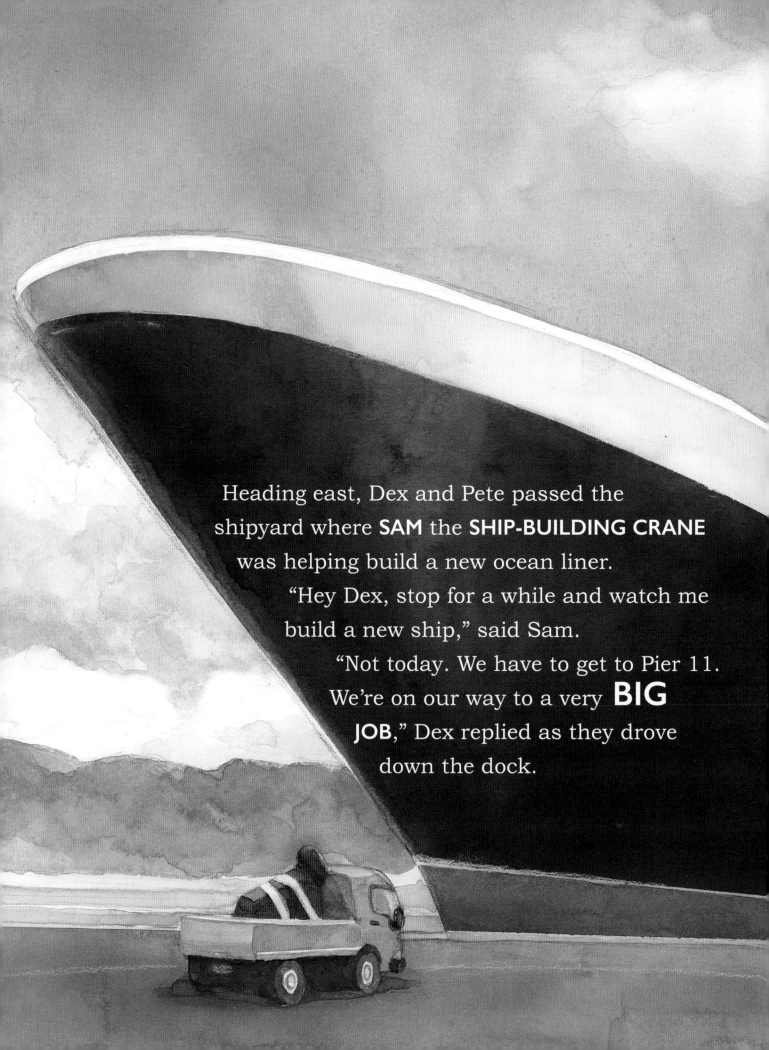

Heading east, Dex and Pete passed the
shipyard where **SAM** the **SHIP-BUILDING CRANE**
was helping build a new ocean liner.
"Hey Dex, stop for a while and watch me
build a new ship," said Sam.
"Not today. We have to get to Pier 11.
We're on our way to a very **BIG
JOB**," Dex replied as they drove
down the dock.

Dex and Pete finally reached Pier 11. **SALLY** the **SHIP-TO-SHORE CRANE** lifted Dex onto a ship heading across the waters.

"Have a great trip!" Sally yelled as the ship left the dock.

After days crossing the quiet ocean, Dex heard
the sounds of offshore cranes at work!

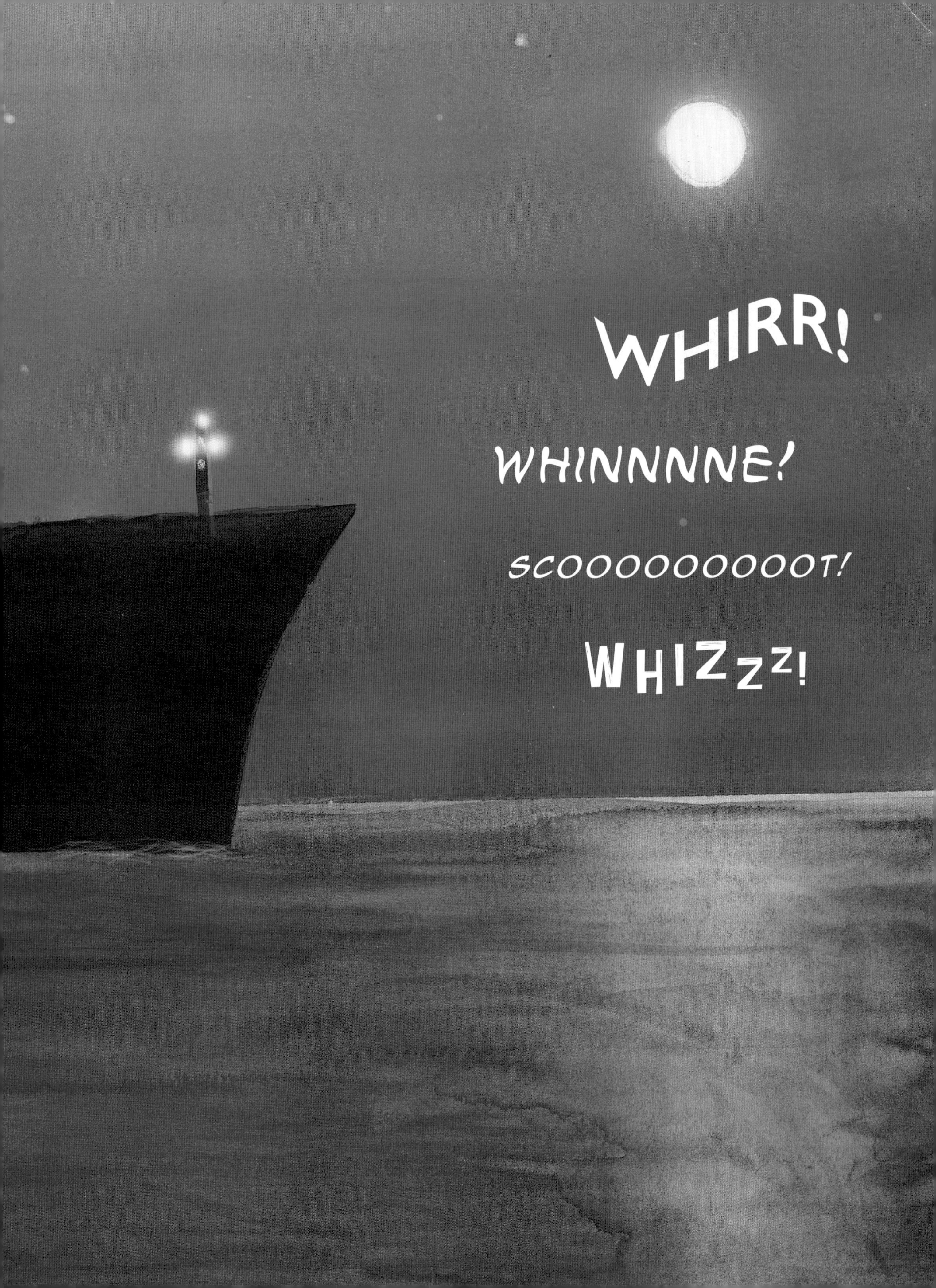
WHIRR!
WHINNNNE!
SCOOOOOOOOOOT!
WHIZzz!

It was a giant **OIL RIG**! Like an island of
CRANES in the middle of the ocean, the oil
rig extracted oil from under the seabed.

Nearing land, Dex passed a
FLOATING CRANE installing a
new section of a bridge.

"*Toot-Toot!*" hooted the floating
crane.

Back on dry land, a massive 18-wheel
MOBILE CRANE zoomed by Dex and Pete.
"*Beep-Beep*! Welcome to the big city,
little fella!" honked the 18-wheeler.

Driving through the city, Dex had never seen so many cranes. Giant **TOWER CRANES** were busy helping to construct tall skyscrapers.

Coming Soon
City Center

Dex wondered, "Did someone make a mistake? What can I do in this big city?"

Soon, Dex and Pete arrived
at a beautiful building with
huge marble columns.

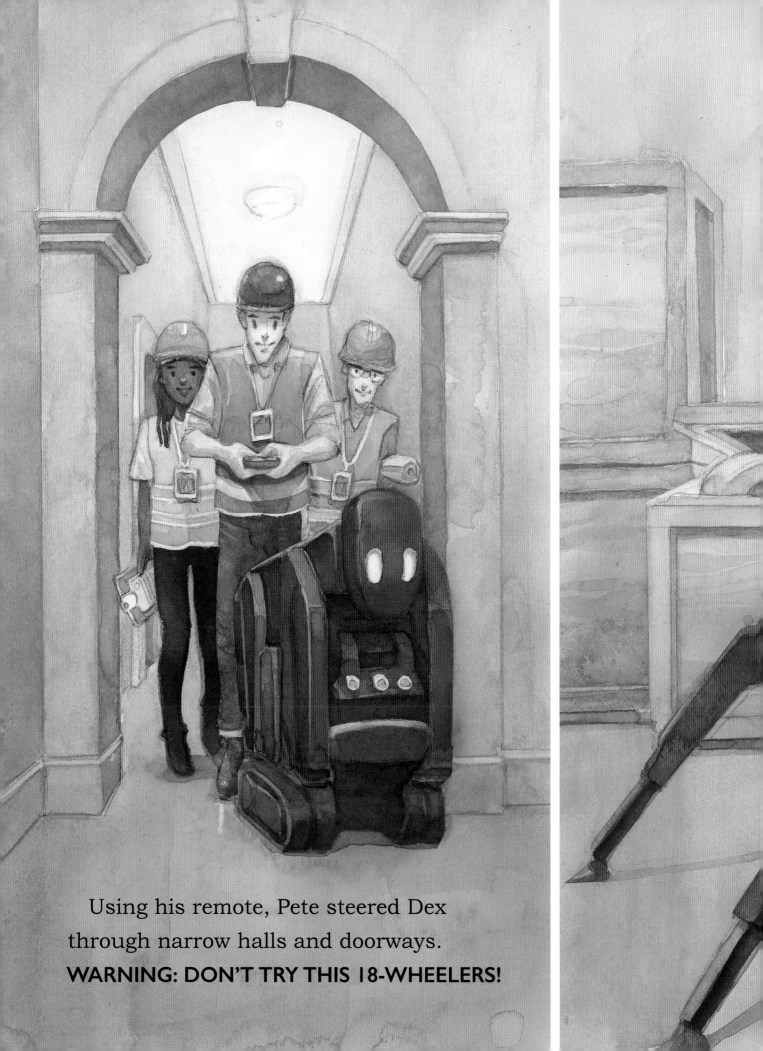

Using his remote, Pete steered Dex through narrow halls and doorways. **WARNING: DON'T TRY THIS 18-WHEELERS!**

AHHHHH!

Dex entered a large room containing lots of crates. At last, he could unfold and stretch his long legs.

One by one, Dex gently removed the pieces out of the crates . . .

and lifted them high into the air where workers put the pieces together.

Though small, Dex is strong
enough to lift a ton. (That's
2,000 pounds!)

Finally, Dex and Pete stepped back to admire their handiwork. They had just helped put together a . . .

TYRANNOSAURUS REX!

"A **BIG** JOB well done!" said Pete.
Dex couldn't agree more.

FUN FACTS ABOUT CRANES

A **LOADER CRANE** (also known as a Knuckle Boom Crane or Truck-Mounted Crane) is a truck or trailer fitted with a bendable power crane arm. Loader Cranes are often used to transport equipment or materials. The operator uses the crane arm to load and unload materials for the workers.

Strength: Loader Cranes used for transport can carry loads up to 20 tons. That's almost 10 cars!

A **TELESCOPIC CRANE** is a crane with a telescoping boom, or long arm, that can extend upward as high as 131 feet to deliver materials to workers. Telescopic Cranes are designed to easily travel to a worksite. A **MOBILE CRANE** is a crane with a telescoping boom on a moveable truck platform.

Strength: One particular 18-wheel Mobile Crane can lift up to 1,500 tons. That's equal to lifting 700 cars!

The **SHIP-BUILDING CRANE** (or Shipyard Crane) is part of a family of cranes called Gantry Cranes. A Gantry Crane has two columns connected together at the top by a bridge. Gliding across the bridge is a crane unit placing parts of a ship where they are needed.

Strength: The most powerful Ship-Building Crane in the world can carry 22,000 tons. That's over 10,000 cars!

The **SHIP-TO-SHORE CRANE** (also known as a Container Crane) is also a Gantry Crane. Ship-to-Shore Cranes are used at major shipping ports around the world to load and unload heavy containers filled with everything from toys to kitchen sinks. Ships pick the containers up from one dock and deliver them to another one across the globe.

Strength: Container Cranes can lift from 65 to 130 tons. That's a lot of toys!

OFFSHORE CRANES are cranes mounted on a platform built off coastlines or in the middle of the ocean. Offshore Cranes are used to lift materials and workers from ships to the platform. Most offshore platforms are oil rigs that extract oil from the bottom of the ocean.

Size: Some rigs are as large as a football stadium and weigh nearly 200,000 tons. One rig reaches 9,000 feet down into the seabed!

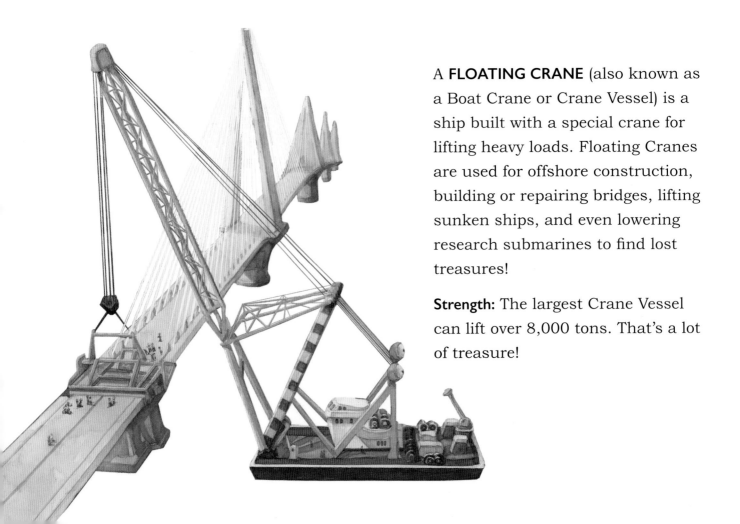

A **FLOATING CRANE** (also known as a Boat Crane or Crane Vessel) is a ship built with a special crane for lifting heavy loads. Floating Cranes are used for offshore construction, building or repairing bridges, lifting sunken ships, and even lowering research submarines to find lost treasures!

Strength: The largest Crane Vessel can lift over 8,000 tons. That's a lot of treasure!

TOWER CRANES can be seen dotting the skylines of many cities, building tall skyscrapers. Tower Cranes do not move; they are assembled at a worksite on a concrete base. Tower Cranes lift tools and equipment up to workers at heights regular cranes can't reach—sometimes they even lift smaller cranes.

Height: Tower Cranes are the tallest cranes in the world, often exceeding the height of the skyscraper they are building. One even stands at 400 feet tall!

MINI CRANES (or Spider Cranes) are small cranes that can fold for easy travel and can work where other cranes cannot. Because Mini Cranes are often used to work on the interior of new buildings and stadiums, the public rarely sees them. Though small, Mini Cranes are very strong.

Strength: The smallest Mini Crane model can fit through a doorway and lift almost 2,000 pounds—just like Dex!

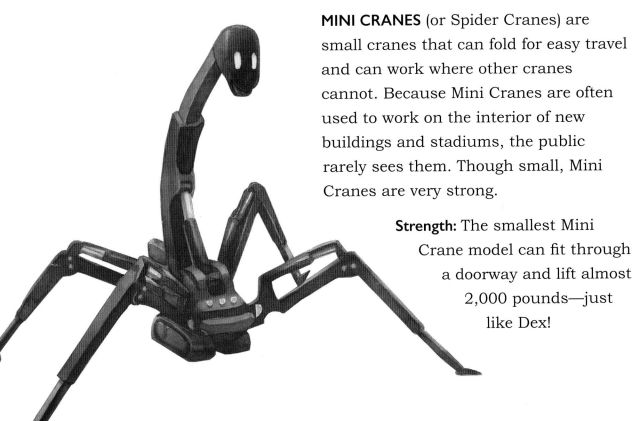